Marriage

for

Convenience

Marriage for Convenience

a Liberian folklore

Jeremiah Tarue Wilson

Village Tales Publishing

LAWRENCEVILLE, GA

Published in the United States by:
Village Tales Publishing
Lawrenceville, GA

A catalog record for this book is available from the Library of Congress:
LCCN: 2019909577
ISBN-13: 9781945408427
eISBN: 9781945408434

Book Layout and Cover by OASS

Printed in the United States

This book is dedicated to:

Prof. John S. Willams

A marriage is a deep and loving friendship, one in which love is strong that each would sacrifice for the other.

FOREWORD

An adjunct writer of stories, this book is a manifestation of Jeremiah Wilson's vision for cultivating the minds of Liberians, and challenging them in becoming writers. By becoming writers Liberians will meaningfully participate in the Liberians education, especially the youths, the efficient sector. This will acquire a cultural change; especially the culture of dependency that has made many educated Liberians think that Liberians cannot do what others can do.

This is a story about giving your best and especially doing whatever you can do to help others, one of the important concepts of the author. I am quite impressed with this book. This is a good beginning for a nation coming out of civil war and a devastating Ebola disease outbreak.

I hope students and other readers will support Wilson's vision for Liberia.

Prof. John S. Williams
Professor of English (*University of Liberia*)

Chapter 1

Marie's beauty, power, and wealth surpassed all, even becoming the perfect partner to fulfill most men's fantasy. People wondered most about the source of her wealth, or what she did for a living. But, only Marie understood the source of her wealth. She had loved the prosperous lifestyle of her rich friends and wanted to be like them; not knowing the cost of such a lifestyle. And since she was so desperate, her friends introduced her into a cult well known for prosperity, but at the cost of blood sacrifice—a human's life.

Marie obtained her membership in the cult, committing to their laws; of course, keeping it a secret from her husband and family. She lied about everything that would link her to such an organization, telling her family that she simply had business contracts as her friends. They believed Marie's explanation since they had all lived in the shed of poverty all their lives. When the time came for Marie to pay for their prosperous lifestyle, it meant two of her children must die. She did not want to go back to a life of poverty; two children died.

The next, and most striking demand came three years later; Marie's husband and their only son had to die. Importantly, their deaths were not to raise suspicion, alarming foul play. Whether it was good, or bad luck, the accident claimed the lives of Marie's husband and their son. While traveling to a friend's party, a truck collided with the taxi carrying them. Marie survived with only bruises. As expected, sympathizers mourned with her and consoled her.

Like a red rose in a garden community of weeds, Marie's life transformed quickly. Promotions at work took her from one position to a higher one, then another, until finally reaching the top position. She soon became the third richest woman in the country.

Now there came a time when the prices of things in the country went sky high; such a time when ordinary citizens sometimes went to bed with an empty stomach. On the other hand, government officials and other rich people had everything they wanted and more. Of course, this led to a riot by angry protesters, which almost ended up into a civil war. As a saying goes, "A hungry man is an angry man." Unfortunately for the rich people and government officials, they were targeted during the riot. As for Marie who was among those targeted, she lost her life to the hands of a wicked protester.

As the last breath left her body, Marie had put all her magical powers in a piece of special jewelry; a diamond necklace. She loved this diamond necklace which she wore on special occasions. Marie never thought it possible that she could part with the necklace.

"All my years of suffering... all the sacrifices I've made, are to get into this necklace," Marie said, putting a spell of misery on the necklace. "Any man or woman, whosoever wear this necklace, shall become invisible. And, the only way to be free from this spell, that person is to get married. No one would marry an invisible person."

Protesters looted Marie's house; stealing her cash and many expensive belongings, including the diamond necklace.

Chapter 2

Whatever came in Tyee's possession, he invested wisely, becoming very successful. People loved him for his generosity, and Tyee had many friends. A lot of women easily fell for him, quickly turning Tyee into a womanizer. However, most of these women followed him for his money. His family was against this womanizing attitude, especially Charlaty his mother, who kept his feet to the fire about marriage. Charlaty irritated him almost every day; every minute they would spend together.

She said to him one day, "My son, I have illustrated all the good things I want you to live by. I've been married long, even before you were born. Get marry son, it takes a real man to prove his maturity by getting married. Settling down would reduce the risk of contracting any sexually transmitted disease that is on the rise. A hint to the wise is quite sufficient."

Having heard enough, Tyee took his mother's advice into consideration. He thought it wise to choose a fiancée among his many women followers, and get married. He would choose a preferable woman, Louisa; also pronouncing his wedding day only three days away. A blissful Charlaty hugged her son, shouting joyful praises.

Three days seemed like a minute in the eyes of Tyee's mother. She happily told her son, "Pretty soon, you would be referred to as a married man."

All who were to attend the wedding were present, setting eyes on both Tyee and Louisa as they slowly march to the stage for their marriage ceremony. But Halfway to the stage, Tyee realized that he had forgotten the jewelry set put aside for him to wear on his wedding day. He did not recognize the person, it was sudden. He could not even remember if it had been a man or a woman, but the kind person appeared suddenly and dressed Tyee with his jewelry, including his favorite diamond necklace.

No one noticed how long it took because it happened fast. People stared blankly where Tyee had been standing, with wide, shocking eyes. Then, Everybody, at the same time, noticed he wasn't there anymore. His closest friends repeated how suddenly he had disappeared. Many took to their heels, especially women and children; some men too. As panic grew stronger among the people, Tyee looked at his mother to make sure she was okay. Then he saw Charlaty's panicked face as she slowly went down to the floor in front of everybody. Out cold; she had fainted.

Everyone began moving and not touching Tyee even though at the point of touching. He watched some men pick up his mother and carry her out, perhaps carrying her to the hospital. Tyee hurriedly followed them out, got in his car and sped after them.

Having to catch up, or keep up, Tyee increased his speed, driving beyond the speed limit. This drew a policeman's attention. The officers got close enough to see the driver. However, it appeared the car had no driver even though it was being driven at high speed. The officers abruptly ended their pursuit and ran the opposite direction.

A bit confuse, Tyee wondered why they had ended their pursuit. He could see them looking at him.

"Am I really invisible?"

He continued the chase because knowing where they were taking his mother was more important.

Tyee reached the hospital, rush in and began asking the nurses for information about his mother. Each person he asked would run away rather gave an answer. It was like he could see them, but no one saw him. They only heard his footsteps and his voice and took off running.

The next best thing to do was drive back to the event hall to see what was happening. Tyee parked a little distance from where a small crowd had gathered outside. He got out of the car, quietly closed the door and walked to hearing distance from the crowd.

"The evil that men do lives after them," someone said.

"It was an evil person who didn't want to see Tyee get married," another responded. "They made him invisible."

Tyee could not make anything of it. He decided to go home. He reached home, went to the living room and sat. A few minutes later, in walked Charlaty and Louisa. Louisa plunged in the chair and folded her arms across her chest. She seemed angry.

Chapter 3

It was a feeling that no matter how hard she tried, Louisa just couldn't understand anything.

"If it were not the grace of God, by now I could have been the loser," she said. "Can you imagine getting married and not be able to see my husband? I thank God that he did not put the ring on my finger. I would have been caught in the middle of nowhere. In fact, from today, no one... absolutely no one should ever call me Tyee's fiancée. It would be an abomination for anyone to call me that. No one should ever call my phone, or ask for me, I am not part of your family."

Louise finished and hurriedly walk out, leaving Charlaty alone. "Why me, God?" she cried, looking toward the sky.

In the main time, Charlaty, highly irritated, sat searching in her mind for possible solutions. She hated the fact that her son's marriage did not come to be. Call it despair, but this was something that hurt Charlaty more than anything.

"The best thing now is the worst thing," she reasoned with herself. "The best thing was to get married, but now the worse thing has happened."

It was more than crying, it was the kind of trouble sobbing that comes from a person drained of all hope. Charlaty did not see anyone, but she recognized Tyee's voice. She too started crying.

A mother's crying usually worries her children, and this time was no exception. Charlaty's other children gathered around to comfort her, as well as help find a solution. They accepted the shift of focus onto Tifhan, Tyee's younger brother. He would be sent to Nyenawliken and visit with Nyenswah, priest of the god of invisibility. Nyenswah possessed the power to see invisible things, so Tifhan was to make an inquiry.

After a long journey to Nyenawliken, Tifhan came face to face with the Oracle. It was rather a voice that greeted Tifhan when he entered the area of the oracle.

"Who are you?" the voice asked.

It was low, with a trace of huskiness and a hint of more power than anything Tifhan knew.

"I am Tifhan. I've come from Pleebo," he responded. "I am seeking a solution to a problem. I have come to see you."

"You cannot see me," the voice said. "But you have seen a clear picture of my shrine. You cannot go back home safely until you follow a simple rule. That is the only way you would be able to see me."

Tifhan nodded.

"Listen, right where you are, remove your shoes. Walk backward, slowly through the entrance. And after you have entered the shrine, there is a chair planted in a white circle. It has gamble seeds on it, sit in that chair and wait for me."

Tifhan did as instructed, sat in the chair and waited.

At first, it was as soft as a whisper and grew in intensity until it was right next to Tifhan's ears. There was a howl, whining noise, enough to raise the hairs on his arms. Then, the oddest thing suddenly appeared, a monstrous nature of the creature. Tifhan tried to get up and run, but the power of the creature kept him tightly planted to the chair. At that moment, amazingly, the creature's form reduced in size and height to a normal man. Nyenswah appeared.

"Truly, you are from Pleebo," he said. "I usually don't have many guests, especially at this time. However, you look worried. What problem brought you here?"

"If a hunchback man says, 'behind me is not looking good'," Tifhan said, "he is not talking about the hunchback, but the problems that are on his mind that are pursuing him every minute of his life."

Nyenswah nodded.

"Unfortunately, my brother, Tyee, became invisible during his wedding ceremony. This problem has shaken up our entire family. And the saddest thing is, we can hear him whenever he cries, but we cannot physically see him. I have come to ask for your advice and to find a solution. My mother, especially, is so heartbroken, it's like she's dying."

"I have the powers to do just what you are asking," Nyenswah said. "Look in that mirror," he pointed, "I'm about to invoke him in it. Do not talk until I tell you to do so."

"Ba ba ba pa pa ple ple!" Nyenswah started his incantations. "Now, you can talk," he instructed Tifhan when he finished.

But, there was no image in the mirror.

"What happened," Tifhan asked.

"The spill your brother is under is strong and powerful," Nyenswah said. "His spirit can only be invoked at night."

"What are you going to do?" Tifhan asked.

"I will tell him I am the god of invisible things," Nyenswah replied. "Do not talk again until I tell you to. I will turn my shrine extremely dark, then try to conjure him. When he appears, question him." Nyenswah said.

Ba ba ba pa pa ple ple! Nyenswah's incantations continued again.

The entire place turned to black darkness. Tyee appeared in the mirror.

"What caused you to become invisible," Nyenswah asked.

"I do not know," Tyee replied.

"Tifhan, now you can ask, " Nyenswah instructed.

Chapter 4

"Brother, do you have any solution to this problem?" Tifhan asked.

"If I have any solution, I would be the one giving you instructions," Tyee replied. "I am still just a human being. I do not have extra powers to find things out. You cannot see me or touch me, but I see all of you. I see how you cry for me, especially Mother."

Tyee's eyes filled with tears.

"He has to go," Nyenswah interrupted.

"No! No!" Tyee pleaded. "Please, we are not done. I want to see him... I miss him. Please, please allow me to see my brother."

Tyee's mouth formed the briefest of sorrow before he was gone.

"What can we do?" Tifhan asked.

"This problem is not an easy one," Nyenswah said. "Go home and find out what caused the problem. When you do, come back, and I will find the solution. I do not have the power to find out what caused the problem. If you know the cause of the problem, I can find the solution."

Tifhan nodded.

"I invoked him because I thought he knew the cause of his problem. Unfortunately, he did not know. Neither do you. I am limited now. Go and find out. Come back, and I will be willing to help you. Go in peace, Tifhan."

The long return journey took Tifhan back. By the time he got home, night had fallen and enveloped Pleebo in a blanket of darkness. The family was beyond excitement to embrace him and catch up on the news he had brought. As tired as he was, they peppered him with questions rather than allowing him to rest.

"Did you see Nyenswah?"

"What did he say?"

"Did he tell you what happened to Tyee?"

"What was his advice?"

Charlaty joined the family and greeted her son. "Our ears are set to listen to all Tifhan has to say, but he is tired," she said. "Let's give him time to rest."

After a very short rest, the family gathered around Tifhan to hear all about his visit with Nyenswah. But Tifhan sat with a face of utter defiance as if he were waiting for a daring challenge. Something flashed beneath the surface of his hardened expression.

"Tifhan, we are here to listen," Uncle Wion said. "Say exactly what Nyenswah told you."

Tifhan remained quiet.

"Are our ears too small to hear what you have to say?" Uncle Wion asked.

"You have not caused this misfortune," Charlaty said. "Feel free to say whatever you have to say."

"Or, is the horn too heavy for a cow to bear," Uncle Wion added.

"A mute man is only happy for his condition when he is faced with difficult questions," Tifhan said. "Or face with interrogation that will either convict him for a crime committed. At the same time, he is sad about his condition when he has the chance to express his love and affection to a special girl that he really loves."

"A mute man," Uncle Wion said incredulously. "We sent you on a mission... you had a task to perform for us, and we want to know how it went."

"Yes... yes," some family members said, nodding their heads.

"I'm not a mute man," Tifhan said. "Although I am happy in my muteness. At the same time, I am sad for the condition I am in. I want to say it, but don't know where to start."

"If Tifhan is not ready to talk, then I am going," Uncle Wion let out his frustration. "He cannot just hold us here for nothing."

"Why is Uncle Wion taking this so personal," Tifhan asked. "As if I am responsible for what happened."

"Tifhan, there is no time for sharing the blame," Charlaty said. "Let's forget the argument." Then she turned to Uncle Wion and said, "Wion, please don't go. One tree cannot make a forest... we have to work this problem out together as a family. No one should be a bone of contention."

Charlaty hoped she had cool down the tension. She smiled when Tifhan started to talk.

"Yes, I met Nyenswah," Tifhan started.

This got everyone's attention.

"He told me that I should come home and find out what caused Tyee to become invisible," Tifhan continued. "Before that, Nyenswah invoked Tyee in an object that looked like a mirror."

This drew intense stares.

"He appeared," Tifhan assured. "We asked him questions, then I personally asked him whether he knew the cause of his problem. Unfortunately, with tears in his eyes, he did not know."

"Mummm," the whole family whined in one melodious voice.

"One tree cannot make a forest, right?" Tifhan said, looking at his mother. She nodded. "So, we have to work on this problem together."

The family nodded in agreement.

"This is where we stopped," Tifhan continued. "Now, we have to move forward. In fact, we must move forward fast because I saw Tyee and he is not well."

Everyone gripped with this news.

"We have to stop crying," Tifhan said, again, looking at his mother. "Rather than cry, let's find a solution."

"Thank you, Tifhan," Uncle Wion said. "You have taken up our task and brought back results. Now, we must take the bull by the horn. We will send you back... not to Nyenswah this time. We will send you to Jokoken to meet Nyenkan, a soothsayer, who is omnipresence. He is the best person who can help us now."

Family members supported the idea of sending Tifhan back.

Chapter 5

"The journey to Nyenkan is not a short one," Charlaty said. "If Tifhan agrees to go, he should not go alone. I do not want to lose another child."

"I agree to go, Mama," Tifhan said. "I will go alone. Nothing will happen."

The long journey started. Tifhan complained of the uneasiness of the journey but had courage from beginning to end. He had reached a place that should have been Nyenkan's shrine, but Nyenkan had moved to a new place. Tifhan spotted a kola nut tree, sat down and lay against it to rest.

"Is this a dead end," he thought out loud to himself.

Tifhan had realized that those who come to Nyenkan's territory must see him in order to remember the way back. Nyenkan is the only person to show the way back. Fear found Tifhan, and he got scared. He began crying, thinking he would be no more.

A lullaby, like a soft wind, came from nowhere. The singing was like oil spilling all over one's soul, or like a pair of loving arms of a beautiful woman wrapped around you. Tifhan imagined it could also be the voice of a mermaid easily willing to harm him.

Tifhan thought to say his last prayer and looked up. Without any detectable noise, a snake was making its way down the kola nut tree toward him. The snake's gaze fixed on him, a dark tongue flitting into the air every few seconds, sensed Tifhan's fear. Tifhan got up to run.

"Don't run," the snake said.

Tifhan froze to the mystery of a talking snake.

"People do not cry here," the snake said. "Are you afraid of me?"

Tifhan nodded.

"Do not be afraid of me, I am a human like you. I was changed into a snake. My best friend and I came to Nyenkan for the medicine to attract men. We were given the medicine pot, but just as we were leaving, the medicine pot dropped. It shuttled, and the medicine wasted. The medicine was destroyed, and this made Nyenkan angry. He punished us by transforming me into a snake, and my friend into an anteater. My duty is to carry people to his new shrine and my friend's duty is to eat the ants that come around to destroy his medicine. I won't harm you, so do not worry," the snake assured.

Tifhan took in his breath and let it out slowly.

"How long is your punishment?" he asked.

"Five years," the snake replied. "We are now serving our last five months."

"What's your name?"

"Teneh," the snake replied.

"And your friend's name," Tifhan asked.

"Her name is, Massah."

"Would you take me to Nyenkan?" Tifhan asked.

"Yes," the snake replied. "I will take you to his new shrine, but you must follow my footprints."

"Your footprints," Tifhan said incredulously. "Does a snake have footprints?"

"Nyenkan gave me footprints," the snake said.

"Okay," Tifhan said, "I am ready."

"When we get there, you must enter the shrine backward," the snake warned. "Then, sit on the bench that is covered with green leaves and wait for Nyenkan. Let's go."

The snake moved in front of Tifhan and hinted him to follow. Step by step, Tifhan followed the tiny footprints between him and the snake until they reached the shrine. Then, he made his way to the bench covered with green leaves, sat, and waited.

Chapter 6

Nyenkan appeared suddenly like lightning would lit the skies.

"What chased you here," Nyenkan greeted Tifhan. "You look worried."

Tifhan replied with a parable, "A toad does not run in the daytime for nothing."

"That, I know," Nyenkan agreed.

"I am like a tortoise that has a fire on its back," Tifhan said. "Until the fire is quenched, I have no rest. But the big question is, who will quench the fire on my back? The fire is severe as if I am taking acid for water."

Nyenkan nodded.

"This is the reason I am here."

Nyenkan cleared his throat and said, "Our traditions and ancestors prepared this shrine as a place where we seek solutions to our problems. You have just put a burning heart in cold water. Tifhan, do you know me?"

"I do not know you," Tifhan answered.

"I am omnipresence and omniscience," Nyenkan said. "I am a god to those who bring their problems."

Then Nyenkan chanted, "Ple ple ba ba! Our people say that the rain that falls in the forest does not stop soon. Until you cut down the trees from over you, before its leaves will stop dropping water on you."

"What do you mean?" Tifhan asked.

"It is a long story," Nyenkan said. "But, to cut a long story short is always the best thing to do."

Nyenkan chanted the story.

"Once upon a time, there was a severe hunger in the town and people went on into a riot. Some looted other people's properties. Tyee, your brother, with some other boys went to a very rich woman's house and looted her properties. They did not know this woman had a ritual. While looting, one of the boys killed the woman. Before she died, she put woe on a beautiful diamond necklace that she had. And, anybody who wears the necklace would become invisible. Unfortunately, that was the necklace your brother wore at his wedding. Now, the only solution for his invisibility is to get married."

"Who can marry an invisible man, Tifhan asked.

"This is the question you should answer," Nyenkan replied. "Go in peace, Tifhan, and solve your problem."

Like he entered the shrine, Tifhan walked out of the shrine backward. The long journey back home became much shorter, as he had double his steps.

"Mama! Oh, Mama," Tifhan cried when he reached home.

Everyone ran out of the house to greet Tifhan. Happy to see her son, Charlaty greeted him with a big and long lasting hug.

"Let's all sit down," Tifhan requested.

In no time, the entire family sat in a semicircle before Tifhan.

"We are staring at you like we did an old story-teller in Kellepo," Uncle Wion said. "He used to bring the children out whenever the moon shines to tell them stories. But one day the children ran out when they saw the moon shining, not knowing that the old man was sick. As soon as they brought him out of his hut to their meeting place, the old man's walking stick broke. He had laid all his weight on it being weak. The old man fell down and died. Now, it is often said in Kellepo that storytelling killed him."

"Since we are staring at you, Tifhan, like the way your uncle put it," Charlaty said, "you have a story to tell us. Hopefully, it is a good one."

"I have a new story," Tifhan replied.

"New to our ears?" Uncle Wion asked.

Charlaty said, "Then, go ahead, we are listening."

"The necklace that Tyee wore on his wedding day made him become invisible," Tifhan said.

"How come?" Charlaty asked. "How can a piece of jewelry do that?"

"It is not an ordinary jewelry," Tifhan said. "Not what you would take it to be. Do you remember the time of the state of emergency?"

Everyone nodded, confirming the incident.

"Those boys we heard about, that looted the people's properties, killed a very rich woman," Tifhan said.

"Is she the woman we heard about while we were still in Gbartarmu?" Uncle Wion asked.

"What woman?" Charlaty asked.

"The one that was murdered in her house," Uncle Wion said.

"Yes," Tifhan answered. "That's her."

"I am still trying to understand how she became our problem," Charlaty said.

"She put woe on the necklace before she died," Tifhan informed. "Anybody who wears it, that person will become invisible, as the woman had a ritual."

"But, how did Tyee get it?" Charlaty asked.

"I'm sorry Mama," Tifhan said. "Tyee was part of the boys that looted the properties. All that we are enjoying today are from the woman's labor."

"I knew it," Uncle Wion said, shaking his head. "I suspected the riches Tyee accumulated was in such a short time. I've always had bad feelings about his wealth."

"You said nothing about your bad feelings as long as you were getting money from my son," Charlaty rebuked Uncle Wion.

"This problem is complicated," Tifhan cautioned, attempting to calm everyone down. "The solution to this problem is, Tyee must get married while in his invisible state."

"How can this happen," Charlaty said, bursting into tears. "Who would want to marry someone they cannot see?"

"That's why we need to work together," Tifhan said. "We must put our ideas together and work as a team."

"Remember, Tifhan, when you came from Nyenswah, you said that if we find out what the problem is, he will help us with the solution," Uncle Wion said. "I think it would now be preferable if you could return to Nyenswah."

"You are right, Uncle Wion," Tifhan said. "I think we are at the end of this problem. A bad sore needs bad medicine. I will go to see Nyenswah again."

Chapter 7

The solutions to problems are good, but a timely solution is much preferable; for time is irreplaceable, and time is of the essence. This made Tyee's family be time conscious. Charlaty bided him farewell and a safe journey from the heart of a mother that wished to hear good news when he returns.

As Tifhan continued his journey, he thought about the good times and the bad times he had with his elder brother. He remembered one time when they were both much younger when their father died and their mother had nothing to offer them, they suffered to get even food to eat. What really brought sorrow to him was how Tyee's life was almost lost because of him.

It happened one evening while coming from the farm as they were crossing a river on a long log stretching from one side of the river to the other side. Tifhan slipped and fell into the river. He did not know how to swim. Knowing there were crocodiles in that river, without a second thought, Tyee jumped in the river after his younger brother and rescued him. He knew he had been lucky not to have been eaten by a crocodile, but its tail had rubbed against Tyee's leg and left nasty gashes.

Tyee came out and said to his brother, "Let's go home, Tifhan, Mother might be worried about us. We should be thankful to the gods of the river, they delivered us."

Tifhan increased his steps.

Now Tifhan felt willing to make the sacrifice for his brother. He was careful to follow all instructions before entering Nyenswah's shrine.

"I have come back, Nyenswah," Tifhan greeted.

"Have you diagnosed the problem," Nyenswah inquired.

"Yes," Tifhan answered.

"So, what is the problem?"

"Tyee must get married in his invisible state," Tifhan replied.

"That would be hard," Nyenswah said. "Girls of these days are realistic."

"This is the reason I'm here."

Nyenswah nodded and began his ritual. Tifhan watched him chant and throw gamble seeds repeatedly on a mat made of lion skin on the floor. He ended the chant and handed Tifhan a raffia bag.

"In this bag is a mirror, a piece of chalk made of clay, and green herbs," he told Tifhan. "They are the solution to your problem. Use the chalk and sketch reflection you want to see in the mirror, then say the name out loud. If you want to see your brother, for example, sketch a human and call his name. He will appear in the mirror. You can talk to him then."

Tifhan nodded.

"But, a female must never see the mirror with an image on it," Nyenswah said.

"My family is grateful for your help," Tifhan said. "I will follow all of your rules."

"A grateful spirit is always a good thing for people to have," Nyenswah said. "Because you have such a spirit, you can call on me at any time in case of future problems. I will help you. Go in peace, Tifhan."

Tifhan left Nyenswah's shrine the same way he entered; backward. On his way back home, he thought about the possibility of a working solution. The idea of practicing Nyenswah's instructions came to mind.

Chapter 8

Tifhan didn't have long, but in his heart, he knew the family would survive this problem. This solution attempt was more of a rescue mission than anything else. And, everything was centered on following Nyenswah's rules.

He sat under a tree in the warm breeze of a dry season evening. Tifhan took the mirror and piece of chalk out of the raffia bag. Then, he drew an image of a man while he called his brother's name, "Tyee!"

Tyee appeared in the mirror.

"Tyee," Tifhan said incredulously. "I've found the solution to the problem. You are to get married, while still in your invisible state. The question now is, which girl do you know would be willing to do so?"

"I do not know," Tyee replied. "All the girls I hung out with are no longer around. Even if they were, I don't think any would buy into this idea."

"I remember one girl when we lived in Gbartarmu," Tifhan said. "We were very young; we play together. The girl's mother always predicted that you would marry her because of how well you got along. Do you remember?"

"I remember," Tyee replied.

"Do you remember her name?"

"Wonwin," Tyee said.

"Yes, Wonwin," Tifhan confirmed. "Do you think she would be willing to help us?"

"We have not gone back since we left the village in Kellepo. Perhaps by now, she has already been given into marriage."

"We have a better chance with her, Tyee," Tifhan said. "We can tell them that you are abroad, and you have sent us to ask for their daughter's hand in marriage."

"What if she's already married to another man?"

"Then, we can 'steal the cookie from the cookie jar', Tifhan joked. "Seriously, you are invisible. When you become visible, you can send her back to her husband. We have a good chance if she's not yet married."

"What if her parents want to see me?"

"A dead cow should not be afraid of a knife," Tifhan said. "Everything will be fine. It is good that your voice can be heard. I have an idea."

"You do?"

"Yes, we will be doing this by hook or crook," Tifhan said. "These people are illiterate and live far from the city. We will tell them that we are using modern technology that's why they cannot see you, but can only hear you."

"Go on," Tyee encouraged.

"We will select the most recent, and best, photos of you, and distribute them among the villagers, including the girl's parents. They will be observing the photographs while we talk. Before they know it, you would be married and become visible."

"Sounds like a good idea," Tyee said.

"Start thinking about what you would say, Tyee," Tifhan said. "You will need to get the girl's attention. If you can sing, sing well. Do something that will make her want to marry you. The family will collect the money for the dowry."

"Yes, Tifhan," Tyee said, "I think that will be fine. Go home now, so you and the family can decide how soon you will pay the dowry. The wedding must take place as soon as possible."

Tifhan put the mirror and the chalk back into the raffia bag and headed home.

Chapter 9

"Mama! Mama!" Cynamie, Tifhan's sister, screamed. "Tifhan is home! He's back!"

She ran out of the house and hugged her brother.

"I knew you'd be back soon," Cynamie said to Tifhan.

By now everybody had heard Cyanmie's announcement and came out.

"You are always on the watch when your brother travels," Charlaty told her daughter.

"She is our only sister, Mama," Tifhan said to Charlaty. "It is always a concern when we leave home."

"The way you are smiling, Tifhan," Charlaty said, "I'm sure you have good news. Don't you want to rest first?"

"I will rest after I've delivered the news."

The family gathered under the shade of the large mango tree in the yard. Tifhan sat where all could see him.

"The old folks from Kellepo always say, 'Tricky jack says if you see your friend fighting, you would feel like fighting too," Uncle Wion said. "I wish I had enough strength to go for the solution to this problem, and not this child."

"I am no longer a child, Uncle Wion," Tifhan said. "You should not think that I am."

"Tifhan is a grown man," Cynamie defended her brother. "He is not a child."

"We should hear what we've been waiting for," Charlaty said.

"What I want you to know right now is simple," Tifhan said. "We must plan how we are going to pay the dowry for the girl Tyee is to marry."

"How is this going to happen?" Charlaty asked. "Who is the girl? Have you find one already?"

"It's a difficult task," Tifhan said. "I need everyone's trust and courage. We are going to do this by hook or crook. Tyee and I have already discussed it. Wonwin, our childhood friend who still lives in Gbartarmu, is the girl. All we have to do is persuade her. That means, we have to pay a dowry to her parents so they will not accept payment from anyone else."

"Are we going back home?" Cynamie asked.

"Yes," Tifhan answered. "This is what we are to discuss."

"An opportunity to go back to the village and play with few old friends," Cynamie said excitedly.

"This is not about playing with few friends," Uncle Wion said. "It is about having a solution to our problem. Because you are young does not mean you should think like a child. In fact, be careful about keeping our discussion a secret. Remember, even the walls have ears."

"We will make sure that we take enough money with us on this trip," Charlaty added.

"We are going as a team to represent the family," Tifhan concluded. "Uncle Wion, Mother, Cynamie, and I will make up the team."

Chapter 10

"Our team will break into four functionaries," Tifhan instructed. "Everyone will carry on an oversight. Mother will work directly with Wonwin's mother, and the other women of concern. Cynamie will work directly with Wonwin and the other girls of concern, and Uncle Wion will work directly with Wonwin's father and other men of concern. I will work directly with Wonwin's brothers and other boys of concern in connection with Tyee."

Everyone nodded in agreement.

"In case any of us is ask about Tyee," Tifhan continued, "we should say that Tyee went on a business trip abroad and he is coming back home any time from now. But because of the love he has for Wonwin, he thought it wise for us to make Wonwin his better half before somebody else pays her dowry. You may make up any story to back up what we tell them, but remember, it should not contradict our plan. When we arrive, all of you should listen to me while I'm presenting our case to Wonwin and her family. Anything that I say is what everyone will set their basis on."

"What type of wedding are we going to have there," Charlaty asked.

"It is still not clear," Tifhan said. "Since we do not know, we have to prepare for any unforeseen circumstance. Therefore, we should buy and take items that could be used in both traditional and a kwee wedding."

The family was returning home to the same people in Kellepo. Everyone accepted the plan, and the trip for Kellepo began. As it is often said, 'the stranger that asks questions never miss the road.' The team asked many questions until they reach Wonwin's parent's compound, where they were warmly welcomed under an orange tree.

The oranges glowed more colorful than they usually do in the day shine. The branches spread out as if so proud of the bounty they brought and sweetness they have given within each fruit. The orange tree was a beauty that had sprung from simple seeds blessed with mud and rain. And, it was deeply loved by every member of the compound because of its endless services provided them.

"I am Oldman Jargbo," Wonwin's father introduced himself. "And, this is my wife, Buonine."

He offered his guests kola nuts, the symbol for peace, unity and prosperity; a welcoming gesture of a pure heart.

"Why are you here," Oldman Jargbo asked.

"He who offer kola nuts, offer life," Tifhan replied. "May the kola nuts enable us to work in harmony."

Oldman Jargbo nodded.

"My name is, Tifhan," Tifhan introduced himself. "This is my uncle, Wion, my mother, Charlaty, and my sister, Cynamie. From today, may you always remember our names."

Oldman Jargbo and his wife shook hands with everyone before each took a bite at the kola nuts.

Chapter 11

"Allow me to put first thing first," Tifhan said. "We are pressed for time."

"Pressed for time," Oldman Jargbo said incredulously.

"We are here for three important reasons," Tifhan continued. "One, to ask for your daughter's hand in marriage. Two, to pay her dowry, and three, if possible to take our wife along with us. We want the entire ceremony to take three days, starting tomorrow."

"Three days," Oldman Jargbo repeated. "Starting tomorrow?"

"We don't wish to hurry things up," Tifhan said. "But, we have businesses to attend and we have to return before others take over our business."

Nothing is done hurriedly in the country.

"Nowadays, business is done by competition," Tifhan tried to explain. "To save time, we have traveled in three cars. This way, we are able to carry our bride."

"As the saying goes, 'A fish and a bird can fall in love, but they cannot make a home together," Oldman Jargbo said. "May the gods that bring peace and prosperity to a marriage agree to the marriage you are here for. Which of our daughters are you asking for?"

"Wonwin," Tifhan replied.

As custom in their marriage, Buonine leaned in and whispered something in her husband's ear.

"Who is the man that wants to marry our daughter?" Oldman Jargbo asked, thinking it was Tifhan.

"He is not here," Charlaty replied. "We are here on his behalf."

"My brother, Tyee," Tifhan offered. "You may not remember us, but we and Wonwin were childhood friends when we lived here. He is serious about marrying Wonwin, his childhood friend."

Oldman Jargbo sighed.

"If Wonwin comes, she will remember us," Tifhan confirmed. "We spent our leisure time playing together."

Buonine whispered in her husband's ear once more.

"If Tyee wants to marry our daughter," Oldman Jargbo said, "why isn't he here?"

"He is on a business trip abroad," Tifhan informed "He had asked us to come on his behalf because he's afraid someone will come before him. He loves your daughter."

"How can he marry our daughter within three days when he is not here," Oldman Jargbo asked.

"We will be using modern technology," Tifhan replied. "You won't see Tyee, but you will hear his voice."

"It seems fishy," Buonine said instantly, rather than a whisper in her husband's ear; a first time for her. "However, since this is from the horse's mouth, we will believe it."

Tyee nodded.

"Even so," Buonine added, "this marriage agreement is a difficult one, we are by-passing our tradition. For this reason, it will cost you more. After all, we have to satisfy our kinsmen."

All the things accompanying Tifhan and his family made them seem wealthy.

Chapter 12

With many unnecessary activities avoided, things moved forward fast. Tifhan busied himself in a private place, taking the mirror and piece of chalk out of the raffia bag. He sketched a human image and called Tyee's name. Tyee appeared, and Tifhan presented him with a diagram of the plan.

The diagram showed key points of where people would be seated, arrangements critical of avoiding mistakes, stressing the importance of it being the last efforts to make it a success.

"Here is the plan," Tifhan said. "We will create the stage in a triangular format. A red microphone will be placed here," he pointed to the upper right anger. "I will make that no one uses it."

"Sounds good," Tyee said.

"We will distribute all these pictures of you to the audience, and Wonwin's parents," Tifhan continued. "We will make sure Cynamie keeps Wonwin's attention on the microphone. Mama and Uncle Wion are responsible to keep her parents' company, distract their attention away from the program. Then, I will give you a sign to start speaking into the microphone. At the same time, I will also signal to Cynamie to so that she wakes Wonwin. All will happen after the first activities."

"What type of wedding are we having," Tyee asked. "Will be a traditional, or a kwee one?

"We do now know yet," Tifhan replied. "If it is a traditional wedding, then we are all set."

"What if it's a kwee wedding," Tyee asked, concerned.

"If it is, I've already spoken to someone," Tifhan said. "This person is ready to masquerade as a pastor to perform the ceremony."

Tyee sighed.

"Tyee, be ready for everything tomorrow," Tifhan said. "The program will start at 10:30 in the morning."

Tifhan said good-bye to his brother and put the mirror and piece of chalk back into the raffia bag.

At evening, the full moon hung low in the sky. Tifhan and the rest of the team took their rightful places. Sharing Wonwin's bamboo bed for the night, Cynamie told her how the marriage will benefit her once it comes to pass. The marriage would afford Wonwin many things she could only dream of. Wonwin could only imagine how wonderful it would be, to be the first person in their village to possess such wealth. She could not stop wondering.

Chapter 13

Based on Cyanmie's influence, Wonwin was somehow excited that she would be the first person in the village to be married to a wealthy man; by their standards. While Cyanmie's sleep was interrupted by the normal night sounds of animals in the village, Wonwin slept soundly. Wonwin even remembered a song in her dream that she and Tyee sang when they were children.

The village alarm clock croaked at the crack of dawn.

As most preparations were done the day before, Buonine, Charlaty, and Cynamie dressed Wonwin for the first part of the traditional wedding.

"It is only those who prepare and special women are given such opportunity," Buonine told her daughter. "But, it's the wise woman who will make good use of it. Get married, my daughter, I have prayed for such a day to come."

Cynamie recited, "Twinkle, twinkle little star, how I wonder where you are. You are the diamond in my brother's heart."

This made Wonwin smile. Everybody in the room smile.

"It is better to be a diamond in a person's heart," Cynamie said, "than to be dirt in the eyes of others."

Everyone nodded in agreement.

"You are the type of daughter-in-law I have been wishing for," Charlaty said. "I have already accepted you ten years ago...before today. You are the type of daughter-in-law I have been wishing for; I have already accepted you ten years ago before today. You have my blessings, Wonwin. Let's go for you to get married."

"You have my blessings too, my daughter," Buonine said.

"My blessing to you too, my dear sister-in-law," Cynamie said.

The village buzzed with excitement, drumming and singing. People danced like they had forgotten how to stand still. Palm wine and food served in surplus, the villagers celebrated in pure excitement. Then, Buonine, Wonwin, Cynamie, and Charlaty walked into the yard and took their seats; applause spread across the compound.

Chapter 14

Buonine sat by her husband, and Charlaty sat next to her. Wonwin sat between Charlaty and Cynamie. The traditional wedding followed; Oldman Jargbo and Buonine broke the kola nut and gave them to Wonwin, with some palm wine, to serve her husband to be. Tifhan, serving as the master of ceremony, took to the stage. The music lowered and Tifhan made the announcement.

"It is not our tradition for a relative of the groom to serve as master of ceremony. It is always the bride's relative that serves as the master of ceremony because they are the ones who are giving their daughter into marriage."

Thinking Tifhan to be the groom, one wedding guest asked, "How can he be the groom and master of the ceremony?"

"Maybe the groom is not here yet," another guest replied.

"But, there's no time for the groom now," the guest replied. "The bride is now carrying the wine and kola nut."

"Let's watch and see," the other guest said.

Everyone watched Wonwin as she walked to the triangular stage, closely followed by Cynamie. Wonwin walked from one end of the stage to another, but her groom was nowhere to be found. She returned to her father with the palm wine and kola nut. Cynamie patted her back for encouragement, and they ambled back to their seats.

Everyone looked on confused.

"Do not be concerned," Cynamie encouraged. "The day has just begun. In fact, this is only the first part of the ceremony."

Everyone sat hushed with disbelief. Tifhan ordered the drummers to beat the drums, and the singers to sing. He asked that more palm wine and food be served. The guests became alive again.

Tifhan found an exclusive space with his raffia bag, making sure he was not followed. Then, he took out the mirror and piece of chalk, sketch a human image and called Tyee's name. Tyee appeared.

"We missed the first opportunity," Tifhan said.

"I know," Tyee replied. "You also missed part of the first plan."

"What part is that?"

"You forgot to distribute my pictures."

Shock registered on Tifhan's face before he could hide it. Then, a small smile played on his lips.

"Oh, that," Tifhan said. "It slipped my mind. What can we do now?"

"When you go back, tell the man pretending to be a pastor, to drop one ring and hold the other for Wonwin," Tyee said. "Be there to observe the process, and make sure Cynamie is with Wonwin. I will pick up the ring that he drops to place on her finger."

"Okay," Tifhan said.

"The microphone I will be using should be next to the ring on the ground. Let's do this," Tyee encouraged.

Tifhan ran back to join the others at the ceremony. Then, he hurriedly collected the photographs and separated them into three piles. He handed Charlaty one set, and another to Uncle Wion.

"Let's hurry," Tifhan urged. "Distribute these quickly."

Chapter 15

Tifhan hurried the fake pastor to join him on stage.

"The pictures you are looking at are that of the groom," he announced into the microphone.

This drew everyone's attention to the photo they were holding.

The fake pastor dropped the ring, and Tifhan placed the microphone next to it. The invisibility of the holder was absolute, the ring and microphone moved upward with no hands. It made no sounds. The fake pastor attempted to run, but Tifhan stopped him.

"You've been paid for this," Tifhan said.

James, the fake pastor, had no knowledge of the plan. He'd only been paid to pretend to be a pastor.

He had been paid well. Most people thought it was the effect of their drunkenness, seeing the ring and microphone lifted without seeing a hand.

Then, Tyee began singing.

Wonwin suddenly remembered the melody and words to the song. It had been a long time since she heard it. She stood and Tyee continued to sing.

> *"I love you,*
> *Really love you*
> *From the bottom of my heart.*
> *I promise you that,*
> *Our love will never end.*
> *Nothing, oh nothing*
> *Can come between us.*
> *I love you,*
> *My love,*
> *Today and forever.*
> *Your promises that I trust,*
> *I hope this love will never end.*
> *We pray it never dies,*
> *I love you,*
> *My love,*
> *Today and forever."*

The song was the same song Wonwin heard in her dream. It got her attention.

Chapter 16

Wonwin walked towards the singing, followed by Cynamie. Tyee sang the song once more and stop. By now, Wonwin had reached the stage. The ceremony was taking place in the warm breeze of the dry season, yet James was shaking.

His pulse pounding in his chest, fake Pastor James said to Wonwin, "Are you willing to accept Tyee as your husband?"

"Yes," Wonwin answered, "I do."

He looked towards the microphone and said, "Are you willing to accept Wonwin as your wife?"

"Yes, I do," the voice said.

"You can now exchange rings," fake Pastor James said.

No reflections, just a ring moved toward Wonwin's hand and fitted on her finger. She saw no hand to place her husband's ring on his finger, so she held on to it.

"You can kiss your bride," fake Pastor James said.

Wonwin instinctively leaned in to receive her kiss. She saw no one, but strangely, felt a warm kiss. The softness and passion gave the promise of many sweetness to come. Wonwin's lips curled into a smile as if a happy feeling of being alive had taken over her.

"I pronounce you husband and wife," fake Pastor James said.

It was like a spook. An ear-splitting explosion went off; the air became cold and like lightning, Tyee appeared. Tifhan pulled the diamond necklace from his neck right way and tossed it away.

Everything about Tyee was wrong. He had been an attractive youth, but now his face was glistening with sweat, his hair not combed, and mud literally smeared across his forehead. His nails were long and looked like he had not bothered to cut them for months. They were blackened with dirt trapped behind them.

Wonwin's face drained with a shock expressionless stare. She took in his disbelieved appearance and fainted. Oldman Jargbo, Buonine, and Cynamie directed some men to pick up Wonwin and carry her back to the house. Charlaty and Uncle Wion ran toward Tyee and hugged him. Then, they hurriedly took him away.

Oldman Jargbo and Buonine had no idea about the reason for the wedding. It was Buonine's money consciousness they had not asked more questions.

Tyee took a bath, combed his head, changed his clothes and return to the wedding stage. Cynamie helped Buonine come through and accompany her back to the stage. Many of the wedding guests ran off, but a few remained. Tifhan explained to everyone how Tyee's misfortune, and how his brother's childhood love had saved him. There were cheers when Wonwin placed the ring on Tyee's finger, completing the marriage ceremony.

www.ingramcontent.com/pod-product-compliance
Lightning Source LLC
Chambersburg PA
CBHW031903170626
46807CB00004B/1871